Christmas Tales

Adult Short Story Collection

Florian Green

Copyright © 2020 Florian Green

All rights reserved

This book is a work of fiction. The characters, organizations and events portrayed within Christmas Tales have been created for entertainment purposes. Any similarity to real persons, living or dead, is coincidental and not intended by the author.

No part of this book may be reproduced, or stored in a retrieval system, or transmitted in any form or by any means, electronic, mechanical, photocopying, recording, or otherwise, without express written permission of the publisher.

ISBN: 9798574040430
Library of Congress Control Number: 2018675309
Printed in the United States of America

Contents

Title Page	1
Copyright	2
Warning	5
Snow	7
Charity	17
Bonus	31
Espionage	41
Present	48
Flight	58
Sincere Thanks	75

Warning

This book contains sexually explicit material which is not suitable for readers under 18.

If such material offends you, please do not read the stories contained within Christmas Tales.

Snow

~Scotland, Present day~

What a view. Andrew shivered in wonder at jagged mountains marbled in black and white. Their tops reaching far into cloud-swathed sky, they crowned a cotton landscape of blanketed fields and rugged forest. Trees dusted like treats sprinkled in powdered sugar, they lined the sides of the road where he stood ankle deep in fresh snow. He puffed out breath in billows. The air's frosty sting was refreshing but only in small doses.

Pulling his scarf loose, he wrapped it higher around his face and tied it tight at the back, so his cheeks were shielded. Then he unfolded the rim of his woolen ski hat at the back, spreading it downwards. That was better. Still cold as fuck, but better.

Looking both down the hill and back the way he'd walked, he could see the route was clogged with stationary cars. A police SUV with glittering lights was parked in the distance. He couldn't be sure for all the haze and snowfall, but there didn't seem to be a house in sight. The Scottish Highlands were famed for their natural beauty not bustling population, he supposed.

The blizzard was relenting—for now, at least—so he'd taken the opportunity to smoke, stroll and try to find out when the road might re-open. They'd been sitting for hours, and he was certain their 4x4 rental could have handled the weather, had it not been for police barriers.

Now was his chance. A policeman in reflective jacket and cap was coming towards him, plodding up the powdery terrain.

He found it bizarre the police in Scotland didn't carry guns. How did they defend themselves from serious criminals? For him as an American, unarmed cops were ludicrous, but then that was part of the magic of travelling: Observing the quirks of other cultures.

"Good afternoon, officer. Staying warm, I hope?"

The stout man's cherry cheeks bunched into a smile. "Aye, that would be a fine thing. Wishful thinking today though." His accent was harsh but charming.

"Do you have any idea when the road will open? My wife's dying to get warmed up by the fire in Aviemore." Feathery flakes were landing on the cop's cap, smudging the Police Scotland badge at the front in paper thin ice.

He looked around at the white surrounding them and said, "I don't blame her. Bloody freezing out here. But"—he stared down the road and shook his head— "I'm afraid it's looking like an overnight job. Got a truck that skidded into the ditch a couple of miles further on, and the snow is making the bends really dangerous. We need to get that truck pulled clear and wait for ploughs and gritters coming from Aviemore."

"So...?"

Stamping feet, he wiped his sleeves with leather-gloved hands. "Bloody covered in it. I think it'll be tomorrow morning at the earliest before traffic's moving again."

"That's a pity officer, because we have a four by four"—Andrew pointed to their vehicle— "I don't think it would be a problem for us to—"

"I appreciate that sir, but the road's been deemed too dangerous for now. You'll just have to wait." The smile stayed; the eyes had turned a shade sterner.

"Ok, officer. Is there anywhere nearby like a hotel or a pub?"

Face screwing, he shook his head while upturning and clasping the collar of his jacket. "I'd say the nearest hotel is 25 miles at least, and I've been told the snow's got even worse back that way. My advice is don't even think about it. Stay close to your car and keep warm. If you've got whisky, I suggest you pour a few to make the night go quicker."

"I think I'll do just that. Ok, thank you. Oh, and by the way, Merry Christmas!"

∞∞∞

"Anything?" Rebecca was rousing from slumber, swaddled in blankets and with a thick scarf bunched at her neck; she looked adorable.

Andrew closed the door with a heavy thud as he climbed into the SUV's comfortable back seat. "Talked to a cop. He said probably tomorrow morning. There's a truck off the road, too much snow. No chance of leaving until they say so."

"Really? Shit. Then I'm gonna have to—"

"Do your bear impression?"

"What?" She was rubbing her eyes, sitting up. He took off his damp jacket and put it on the front seat; the thick sweater plus snuggling wife was enough for coziness. Adjusting the blankets around him, she cuddled close.

"In the woods, you know."

Letting out a sleepy moan, she gave him a light smack on the arm. "Don't be a jerk. It's freezing out there, but I need to go. Can you come with me, please?"

He brushed back her raven fringe and planted a lip smack on porcelain forehead. "Ok, honey. I'll grab some toilet paper from the trunk."

Wrapped up, they crunched past cars in their search for a suitable way into the forest. He spotted an indentation in the embankment which looked like a small footpath. It led down a slight gradient, all caked in wintry wonder of course. He went ahead, taking cautious steps, holding Rebecca's hand to steady as he guided. "Careful, honey, it's deep. It'll be almost knee height on you."

Once under the trees' canopy, the carpet of root-riddled earth and twigs was dry and easy to walk on. Wood and herb scents caused pleasant invigoration as they scanned for a suitable place. After brushing her lower jeans and clunking chunky ankle boots against each other, she climbed into a sunken hollow behind some bushes. He stood on the other side with his back turned.

"Honey, keep an eye out please."

"Nobody's gonna—"

"And cover your ears."

He started a sigh which ended in chuckle. "Ok, sweety."

A few minutes later he felt a tap on the shoulder and turned to see his wife peering up at him with a broad smile, the lips quivering with shivers. She stepped into his embrace, searching for warmth. "Feeling better?" he asked, enveloping her in his strong arms.

"Yea, phew! So much better. It's cold though. Let's go back and open that coffee liqueur."

"Ok, and maybe put a drop of whisky—"

"Shhh" She paused and held her hand straight like a radio antenna.

"Wha—"

"Shhh. Listen." She broke from him and turned to face the path, which snaked deeper into dark forest.

He stood still and strained his ears. Oh yea. There was a noise. Faint, almost inaudible. Sounded like a bird? A deer? A person? He realized he didn't know what wildlife they had in the Scottish Highlands, and whether it included anything dangerous.

"They don't have cougars or bears or wolves here do they?"

"No, silly. They only have deer."

"You're sure?"

She turned and beckoned him with a flapping white mitten. He stooped, she smooched. "This is why you need to read more about places before we visit them. Now come on, let's go and see."

"I don't know, wandering off into the strange forest to search for a mystery noise when it's about ten degrees out here. Good idea?"

Tugging on his hand, trying to budge his much bulkier frame, she asked "Are you twenty-eight or ninety-eight? Come on."

"I thought you were cold?"

"Walking will warm us up, now come on!"

They trekked further into the forest until it opened onto a small clearing. Flakes were once again cascading in unfettered flurries, covering its flat area. A picnic table and benches sat in the center, layered like a cake coated in rich icing. Maybe 10 feet beyond that was a stream—more of a trickle, in fact—which was unfrozen, and gurgling between frosty rocks and snow-smothered long grass. It flowed underneath an old stone-built bridge with a single arch far broader than the water it spanned.

"I think that might be a Roman bridge," said Rebecca in a hushed voice.

"Why are we whispering?"

She smirked and shrugged. "I don't—"

This time the noise was clear, close. Unmistakable. It was a woman's cry. And not in distress. Rebecca's eyes peeled as her mouth opened in disbelief. "Oh my God. Is that people…doing it?"

"Think so, but where? I can't see. Can you?"

He scanned the trees around the clearing. Nothing. The top of the bridge was empty too.

The sound rang out again, this time in words: "Oh yes!"

She pointed. "Under the bridge. Come on. Be super quiet."

Tensed like intruders on private property, they walked round within the forest's fringe to get a view directly into the bridge's arch.

Oh my. Someone was having fun. A young couple, to be exact.

With their pants and underwear pulled to knees, she was bracing against the wall as he pumped hard from behind. And from her responses, it seemed like the guy was doing a good job. A damn good job. Now *this* was a view.

Andrew got a tug on his sleeve. Rebecca was gesturing for him to join her in crouching behind a thorn bush. She began peering, eyes glinting with mischief. He didn't know what was sexier; watching the live sex or seeing how much it was fascinating his wife.

The man was tall, strong looking; the girl far shorter with glasses and boy cut hair. Only her chubby butt was exposed. Pale flesh was vibrating with each vigorous thrust of her partner's crotch as he hammered with hands grasped on welcoming hips.

He could see the guy had a huge cock, ramming himself in

and out at rapid pace, disappearing between her cheeks like a pumping piston. Her fingers clutched brickwork as he battered away at ass.

And then Andrew felt fumbling down below. Rebecca had taken off her glove and was rubbing his crotch; fondling as she spied on the people screwing. The temperature was still bitter, but his body was warming. He slid his hand under her hat and stroked silky locks while she groped.

The girl's intermittent shouts had solidified into a steady stream of release: "Yes, yes! Oh, oh. Oh, fuck! Oh, fuck! Fuck!" The scene was so animal, primal. Snow tumbling, wood, earth, water; the clouds of cuss-filled puff from their mouths as they climaxed. So hot.

Pants still at her knees, the girl turned and squatted with rear end on full display. She was licking the cum from his cock; completely clean. Collecting drips from the shaft, the girl gobbled with greedy finger sucks.

"Oh my God," whispered Rebecca with her palm still massaging his privates. "She's eating his cum. So hot."

Their fun over, the couple tugged their clothes back into place and walked back along the path towards the road, oblivious of the fact they'd put on a show. Andrew and Rebecca remained crouching and silent until they were out of sight.

They broke into giggles. Now he was standing, she'd moved her hand round to his bottom, enjoying him through jeans. "Let's get back to the car, hmm?"

His dick was throbbing. He couldn't wait. Gesturing to the bridge, he said, "That's closer."

"The car will be warmer, honey."

He shook his head. "I liked what I saw and so did you. We're going under the bridge."

She gritted her teeth and grabbed between his legs. "You having one of your bossy moods?"

Taking gentle grasp of her hat, he claimed a forceful kiss. The lips were relenting, submissive; her eyes were closed when he pulled away. "Get your ass under that bridge."

She gave a tut, but it was lacking in sincerity. "So bossy."

Turning her, he landed a slap on her derriere. Neither too hard nor too light; he knew what she liked. "Move it!"

They passed through the clearing, bombarded by myriads of powdery petals; their icy kisses smothering his face. Rebecca clung tight as they marched under the brick bridge. Once sheltered, he restarted his demands. "Turn around and pull your pants down."

She crossed her arms and pouted in mock rebellion. "And what if I say no?"

He spun her, stood close and hissed, "We're going to fuck. Get those pants down, now."

Reaching back, she stroked his face; her hands were smooth but cold. He'd soon have her heated. Then she unzipped, taking jeans to knees. He took hold of her pink bikini-cut panties and yanked. Her ass looked like a candy apple. Looking back, she said, "Honey, not in my ass. Not without the lube. I'm serious, ok?"

His own lower clothing taken down, he stepped forward and began sliding himself into her pussy, causing her eyes to bulge in surprise. "Does that answer your concerns?"

Breathing heavily, she nodded, already sinking into pleasure.

"Face forward and fuck." He bent her over; she steadied against the bridge's weathered ridges, gasping. Her hips began to push back, knocking his crotch with claps of quivering cheek. "That's it. Fuck. That's what wives are supposed to do, right?"

"Yes"—she yelped as he plunged with a deep thrust— "they are."

They started fucking. His cock was rigid as bone, delving into her snug pussy, hands clamped around soft-skinned hips, bumping, thumping; the weather began to rage in rhythm with their passion. Wind whistled, then howled; the snow dazzling, blasting, as Rebecca coupled with her husband, growling and gasping. Cock and cunt connected by tight unison, he delighted in his dick slipping in and out of his beloved in the slickest of groaning motions.

She was devouring; knees trembling, no longer caring about cold, she pushed back from wall with determined wails. They were like animals breeding, or cave people mating for warmth, seed, freedom, whatever. It didn't matter. This was a wintery Olympus, and they were the gods.

Her moans grew. Becoming fast, high-pitched, the shouts were lost in blizzard battering between trees as she slammed the bricks with palms, squealing, crying, "Fuck me! Yes! Fuck me!"

So, he did. Pummeling with purpose; going in as deep as her passage would permit, he pressed, stuffed, and slammed. Until, stiffening, she loosed a loud, lingering scream, announcing violent release.

She tapped his thigh. "Honey stop a second. Was"—she loosed a panting laugh— "so amazing. You gonna cum?"

"Just about to." He could feel the surge, his swollen cock aglow with nerves teased to the point of tears.

"Step back, let me get down there."

She kneeled in time to catch his first spurts all over chin and cheeks. Opening her mouth, she guided the jets to guzzle their hot, succulent juices of fresh, sticky mineral and salt. Swallowing everything she'd been given; she stuck her clean tongue out as boastful evidence. "All done."

∞∞∞

The rest of the evening was spent on the back seat cuddled under blankets, sipping whisky and liqueur. Exhausted but happy. Laughing, they held each other tight and watched the sky through polished sunroof glass as stormy white darkened to turbulent night. Andrew was glad he had such a wonderful wife.

"How do you like our highlands trip so far?" he asked.

She burrowed into his chest, pulling the fluffy blue blankets higher around them. He could feel her toes caressing the bridge of his foot through thick layered cotton. "Amazing. We need to do it more often."

"Highlands trips?"

"No, outdoor sex."

The next morning, the road opened, and they went on to a cozy chalet and off-piste skiing. Food, music, mountains, people; everything was perfect. But the most exciting part of their holiday remained the thunderous thrills of spontaneity enjoyed in that snowy Scottish forest.

Charity
~New York City, 2009~

Stephen's overcoat and scarf were fending off nature's frosty tickles as he stood at yet another doorstep. Making his pitch, he presented the raindrop-spattered ID which hung round his neck from a lanyard. "Good afternoon, sir. My name's Stephen and I'm collecting donations on behalf of The Christmas Fund for Orphaned Children."

After a brief exchange and mutual Merry Christmas, his collection can was five dollars fuller. Excellent.

Soggy leaves stuck to the sidewalk and cluttered the gutters; scrunched, they mashed together like breakfast cereal soaked too long in milk. He strode over wet slabs, admiring brownstone townhouses and wondering how astronomical their values were. This was prime Manhattan real estate, so God only knew. One thing was certain though: He'd only ever afford one in his dreams.

But that was ok. In a world fraught with hatred and unhappiness, he was content with doing what good he could. In his teens he'd always thought of volunteers as losers, but now he was a man the value of helping others had become clear. A couple of dollars here, five dollars there; it didn't seem much, but it added up. He would knock on every door in New York City if it meant needy kids had even one present to open on Christmas Day.

Arriving at the final house on the street, he stopped to take in its size. Twice as wide as the others he'd visited, it was an elegant structure carved in caramel block and plated with gleaming glass. A broad flight of steps, flanked by ornate balustrade, led to tall double doors; the wood was painted in luxuriant maroon and badged in polished brass. Lights shone from the bulbous bay window on its third floor. Great, he was certain the owners of such a magnificent property would have a dollar or two to donate.

He pressed the security intercom button and waited. No answer. Wedging the plastic collection can under one armpit, he plunged pink hands into his coat's pockets and pulled it tighter. He'd been hoping golden rays might slice through some of the grey.

A lady appeared at the bay window above. She was good-looking, curvy. Dressed in a navy-blue business suit and holding what looked like a glass of champagne, she peered, scrutinizing him from foot to forehead. He presented the can and gave a hopeful smile. She held up an index finger as a signal to wait and then disappeared from view.

With a click, snap, and creak, one of the doors opened. "Hello, young man. How may I help you?" Her sentences were clear, but the words sounded out in mild slur. She leaned against the door frame holding a crystal flute of fizz between manicured ebony fingers; the nails glossed in pastel pink.

He stretched out his charity ID on its lanyard so she could see the photo. "Good afternoon, madam. My name's Stephen and I'm collecting donations on behalf of The Christmas Fund for Orphaned Children. Would you—"

"Orphaned children?"

"Yes, it's a fund to make sure children in the city's orphanages have at least one present to open on Christmas Day. And with just seven days to go, every dollar—"

"That's a very noble cause"—she leaned forward, took hold of his ID and inspected— "Stephen Whittaker. Licensed charity Worker."

Her neck closer to him now, he met floral perfume; syrupy-sweet, it was loud, brash, but pleasing and probably expensive. It blended with crisp grape wisping from red lips as she sipped. He also couldn't help but notice her bust was straining against buttons on the white blouse under her suit jacket. A voluptuous lady, but then he wasn't going door to door to ogle women. This was about the kids.

Stepping back, she gestured for him to enter. "Why don't you come upstairs? We're having a little Christmas party. I'm sure you'll get quite a few generous donations."

"Are you sure? I don't want to intrude."

Her eyes wrinkled in reassurance above an empathetic smile. "Don't be silly. You're not intruding; I'm inviting you. The ladies will be happy to see you. Now come on, it'll give you a chance to warm up too."

Stephen followed her on stairs laid in thick terracotta carpet. Running his hand along the smooth walnut bannister, he enjoyed scents of lemon and vanilla from furniture polish applied in liberal amounts. The staircase reached a landing furnished with a single giant vase before another flight led them towards an enormous open plan living and dining room.

He'd noticed the shape and shift of her bottom while climbing; plump and full, it was pushed tight against what were—he assumed from their sharp fit—tailored pants. It had been right in front of him, so it wasn't like he'd been going out of his way to stare. But it was there. The woman was old enough to be his mother, but he still found her attractive on a number of levels. Nobody liked to admit it—especially him—but money was magnetic, and success was sexy.

And this lady seemed to have an abundance of both. The décor was striking. He had no idea what style or theme an expert would label it, but the sumptuous surroundings conjured images of royal European residences. Luxuriant but not boasting of bling; the half dozen couches and armchairs were silky blue and purple, patterned in gold leaf and positioned on Persian—or maybe Turkish—rugs of coordinating colors, underneath which lay a floor of immaculate marble. Exquisite seascapes framed in shiny lacquer, bright flower arrangements flaring from vases and a grand piano dominating the far corner all combined to majestic effect.

The party was indeed all female. Well-dressed, mature—not one of them looked under forty-five—they were lounging, sipping, chattering, and chirping; glass clinked, champagne bubbled, canapes were nibbled and gobbled as his impromptu host turned to speak with him, extending her hand. "Where are my manners? I'm Isadora. Delighted to meet you, Stephen. Would you like something to keep the chill at bay? Cognac perhaps? Scotch? I have some fantastic bourbon?"

A glittering gold watch hung loose on her wrist, the slender chain slinking forward as they shook hands. "Well, perhaps a bourbon then. Thank you so much."

"You're welcome. Oh, and feel free to take off your coat and relax. Some of my associates"—she raised an eyebrow and gestured towards the other ladies— "might be a little chatty with you, as they've had a few drinks. Don't worry though, they're harmless enough."

"Thank you so much." Taking off his coat and scarf, he hung them over his bulky forearm.

"Here, let me take those for you. And there you go, Kentucky's finest."

He took a sip. Oaky spice and toffee glided down his throat in a silky glow. Overtures of classical music were floating in gentle bow glides and finger plucks. No longer smacked by cold wind, he felt his facial muscles relaxing. It was all very pleasant. Chatter slowed as the room began to focus its attention on him.

"Ladies"—Isadora pointed to Stephen holding his collection can— "this nice young man is Stephen. He's collecting donations for orphans, to give them presents on Christmas Day. I hope you'll give generously."

Pretty fingers reached into purses and handbags. He placed his drink on a brown leather coaster and began collecting the donations. The women were all shades and shapes, but one thing which seemed the same was their casual attitude to money. One by one, they slid fat folds of green bills into the slit of his can, some of which required a firm push to squeeze through. He could see the denominations: 10s, 20s, and even a few 50s. He was delighted.

Compliments about his appearance accompanied the cash. The borderline obnoxious comments—or certainly ones tainted by alcohol—were either given directly or aired aloud as observations while they ate and drank. The consensus was that they found him handsome. He was used to women saying nice things about his blue eyes and muscular frame, so it was nothing shocking.

The final lady he approached, who was wearing a suave double-breasted emerald pantsuit and matching heels, seemed keen on a chat. She appeared to be of South Asian descent. Shiny shoulder-length hair, high cheeks bones and pouting lips combined to make her easy on the eyes. When Stephen presented his collection can she folded and pushed two crisp 100-dollar bills into it, then patted the free space on the couch, asking him to join her. Sitting and leaning, the quality material molded round his hips and lower back. It did feel great to relieve his feet after almost a whole day walking in wintery wind and drizzle.

"I'm Lucille, by the way. I'm one of the senior partners at Dawkins and Trent. Corporate law, not half as exciting as it sounds, believe me. But anyway, it's a treat to have a man join us"—she placed a soft palm on his shirt sleeve, caressing with subtlety— "and I think it's just wonderful, the work you do for vulnerable children. You're a real gentleman." The muddled words said she was past tipsy territory.

"Not to mention gorgeous," said a freckly, redheaded lady

sitting further away, nibbling on the rim of a glass holding gin fizz cocktail—he'd spent two years as a bartender in SoHo—while giving a coy gaze.

Laughter and giggles of agreement echoed through the room. Wealthy women were indulging themselves and he was the entertainment. They'd just donated at least a thousand dollars to charity, so it seemed fair enough.

"Oh, thank you ma'am. You're so kind."

"You're right, Sara. He should be in the movies. And these muscles"—she smiled, gripped his bicep, and squeezed— "are you a gladiator when you're not collecting for needy kids?" asked Lucille.

"Oh no, I just work out regularly. Healthy body, and all that."

All eyes were trained on him; Isadora brought his glass of bourbon and sat in an adjacent armchair. She'd taken her suit jacket off, revealing exactly how bulging her breasts were. She took a more controlled tone. "So, what is it you do, Stephen? Or are you a full-time charity worker?" He got the impression she was trying to steer towards the restrained.

He took a gulp of the caramel colored spirit, feeling its warmth massage his chest and stomach. "Actually, I only do this a couple of times a week. My main job is at Radiance Spa in Midtown."

"Radiance? On 5th Avenue?" Lucille asked as another lady refilled her champagne flute. The pink foam frothed to the top, but she caught it with sucking lips before it spilled.

"That's the one."

"And what do you do there?" asked Isadora.

"I'm one of the massage therapists. I specialize in Swedish, Balinese and Lomi Lomi."

Lucille knocked back a half glass before slipping her shoes off, pivoting on the couch and placing her feet in Stephen's lap.

Right on his crotch. "My feet are absolutely killing me"—she stretched out the syllables in 'killing' like they were elastic— "you don't mind giving them a rub, do you? Since you're a professional."

He could feel her heels pressing against his prick. The women were sniggering, chuckling; even Isadora's mouth had formed into a sly smile when she said, "Lucille, you'll make the poor boy blush. Behave yourself."

"He's not a boy. He's"—she crinkled her toes, rubbing them on his thigh— "how old are you?"

"Twenty-four, ma'am and"—he turned to Isadora and smiled — "it's not a problem, really. I don't mind helping out. You ladies have been so generous, it's the least I can do."

"There, see? He's a sweet young man, helping me with my tired feet"—she gestured to his lap with her eyes— "go ahead, spoil me."

She was wearing sheer black socks. He ran his hands along the smooth, delicate material. "May I take these off?"

"They're just socks, Stephen"—she took a quick glance round at her friends— "they're not my panties."

A ripple of smirks and smiles followed; one woman—perhaps away with the grape fairies—loosed a dirty cackle. He slipped off Lucille's socks to reveal pedicured feet with clear-glossed toenails. Cupping a heel in his palm, he began massaging the soft, warm skin of her sole.

"You're really getting spoiled today," said a plump lady in thick-rimmed rectangular spectacles.

"Mmm yes I am. This man has magic hands. Ladies, you don't want to miss out on this." She parted her thighs a fraction, catching his eyes as they wandered. The husky voice slathered in sleaziness, the pretty feet in his lap; his cock was starting to harden.

"Can you do me next?" asked a lady sat across the room.

"Then me," said another.

It seemed everyone had sore feet.

"Are you ok with that?" Isadora's voice was growing more slurred.

"It's really ok. You've given more money today than I've collected all month. I'm happy to give back."

And so he massaged. Isadora brought two soft white towels and some lotion. After Lucille, the ladies stretched on the couch in turns. Pale, tan, toes tiny and long; the pairs of feet were smooth, pampered, and varnished. The women simpered, stared, rubbed heels along his hard-on; it was far from unpleasant.

The party continued. Eyes glinted, glasses were tipped, nibbles crunched and bubbly guzzled. Until Isadora was the only one whose feet hadn't been treated. Approaching her at the bar area beside the entrance, he asked, "Would you like me to do your feet too?"

She was hesitant. "Uh, well, actually—"

"I'm happy to do it."

"Well, you're so sweet but, actually I was wondering if you could maybe do a full body massage for me? I realize that's probably quite presumptuous, but I have so much tension built up. You'd be doing me a huge favor."

"Sure, I'm happy to. As long as your husband won't be jeal—"

She chuckled, taking his hand in a gentle clasp. "I finalized the divorce from that pig last month. Where do you think all the tension came from? Now let me clear this party before they start breaking things."

"Shall I just undress completely?" Isadora asked before sipping yet again from a chilled liter bottle of spring water.

They were in her bedroom, which continued the apartment's theme of grandiose layout and décor. The bed was big enough to hold a sleepover for three little league teams at once. She'd laid towels and a pillow down the middle of its enormous surface, and was now standing barefoot waiting for his direction.

"Sure, if you feel comfortable, then by all means go ahead. Would you like me to leave the room?" The vibe was of exhibitionism, but he had to be polite and offer.

"We're grownups, Stephen. I'm sure you've seen it all before anyway, being a massage therapist. It's no big deal."

Her quivering grin and averting eyes told him it was a big deal; just an unspoken one.

Nodding in agreement, he picked up the lotion bottle and pretended to read its information label as he heard buttons being plucked and zips rasping. He was curious to see her laid bare. His guess was she'd look nice.

"Ok, I'm ready" she said with a hint of tremble in her tone; the booze-infused bravery was faltering somewhat.

Isadora stood naked as nature with a sheepish smile and enormous breasts. Sagging from lack of support, they hung ample, imposing, timeless symbols of fertility and nurture. Her midriff was soft—a little too much fine dining, perhaps—but the belly and love handles weren't off-putting. She was Rubenesque, healthy, carved in adorable curves of flawless ebony flesh.

She made no attempt to cover, and that wasn't surprising. In his experience with regular spa clients, once women had judged a man gentlemanly, they could be quite keen to flaunt.

Stephen gestured to the bed. "Ok I'll start with you lying on your front if that's ok?"

She lay down as he'd asked, with her head eased on the pillow and hands clasped underneath it. Her voice was half-muffled as she said, "I feel so ashamed of the size of my bottom. It's huge."

The quest for compliments was an indicator. He knew where this was leading. "Hmm, no, I don't think it's huge. It's actually in perfect proportion to your body"—he oozed some lotion onto his palms— "and you should be proud of your shape. It's really quite striking. May I start?"

"Oh, please do."

Spreading the liquid across backs of her calf and thigh, he began sliding his hands across her silky skin in smooth strokes. "Is that ok? Are my hands warm enough?" He knew the answer.

She let out a long sigh. "Mmm its perfect. Completely perfect."

"I'm glad to—"

"And don't be shy about massaging my butt. There's a lot of tension in there"—she turned to meet his gaze— "so do what you like, ok?"

He did just that. Coating curvy cheeks, he kneaded, stroked, and caressed as she shifted, gripping the pillow corners and mumbling moans into white cotton. Her legs began to ease apart, leaving shaven sex on open display; the lips were glistening. Hips gyrating against the bedspread, her gleaming ass and thighs smelled like almond milk and baby oil; the soothing scents whispering of delicate care and adoration.

"Is that ok so far?"

"Amazing"—she reached back and stroked his forearm— "and like I said, do what you like."

"Whatever I like?"

"Whatever you like." Her rear was raised, hips moving up and down in naughty rhythm. Beckoning. His cock was throbbing; greased ass cheeks were quivering, wobbling.

Taking gentle hold of her thighs, he moved his face downwards and started eating her pussy. Lavishing it with slippery licks, he probed, sliding his tongue far inside, feeling the wet, velvety folds part as he kissed and sucked with art.

Isadora was groaning. Now on knees, gasping, she reached back and spread her labia wide apart. "Please don't stop, honey. Your mouth is perfect. Lick all of me."

She was pink as bubble gum. Wedging his mouth into her womanhood, he feasted on tender flesh, trying to push his tongue completely into her welcoming passage. He ate and ate. Gorging, slurping, reveling in gluttony; she squealed and flailed, cried out, wailed. "That's so good honey! Feels so good! So fucking good!"

Flipping onto her back with legs open, she ran fingers through his hazelnut locks before guiding him back to the palace of pleasure. "That's it, honey, lick my clit. Yes, right"—she released a gasp in high pitch— "right there. Yes, Keep licking it, sweety. You're a sweet boy. A very sweet boy. Yes, flick it with your tongue. Flick it, honey. That's it. Oh my God, don't stop"— her voice turned deep, focused— "don't stop. I think I'm gonna, Oh God I'm gonna, I'm gonna—"

Her hands clutched at his scalp as she yelped and seized; electrified, as if struck by lightning. And then the tension faded, he felt the grip loosening as she laughed and said, "Oh God. Oh my. Come here and hold me, gorgeous."

Wiping the sticky liquid from his chin, he lay close and cradled her. "Was it nice?"

Rolling her eyes, she broke into a broad smile. "Nice? Nice? Are you"—she planted a strong kiss on his lips— "serious? You know how long it's been since a man did that for me?"

"Well I—"

"Can we have sex?" She was pressing huge tits against his chest; the thick nipples poking into his shirt. Pungent jasmine, orchid and blackcurrant were pulsing from her neck. Brown eyes were somewhere between begging and badgering. How could he say no?

He nodded. "Do you have condoms?"

"In that drawer. Take all your clothes off, please. I want to see your body; you hot bastard."

Stephen stripped naked. She inspected him, running a hungry tongue between her lips. "Damn, you do like working out, don't you? Mmm that cock is gonna be a tight fit. Yes, good boy, make sure that rubber's on properly; I'm going to work that cock hard, don't want it falling off."

She took the towels off, pulled back spotless white sheets and lay back. Ready.

Naked, all his vascular youth on display, he kneeled with his erect cock so swollen it looked like it would burst the latex. "How do you want it?"

"Missionary. A hard fuck."

"Ok."

He started to nestle his cock head into her cunt, causing her to grit teeth and hiss, "I want to be fucked hard, you hear me?"

"I can fuck hard, don't worry."

She was snarling, eyes savoring his nudity; her fingernails dug into his ass as she fondled and groped. "You're a stud, aren't you? I want you to screw me as hard as you can. Fuck like a gladiator, ok?"

"Gladiator? And you're my mistress?" His pectorals were twitching and so was his manhood as its tip teased her slit.

"Yes, good boy. You've got the idea." He pushed his cock deep into her pussy as her legs wrapped around his lower back, bringing him close. Isadora ran palms down his thick neck and shredded shoulders. "Look at this body. You've got more muscle than a gladiator."

She was snug, moist, a pleasure to penetrate. Grasping his ass cheeks, she pushed with hands and pulled with calves, forcing their connection as tight as anatomy would consent. And it was heavenly. He fucked hard, she simpered, her eyes—wincing with the wonders of their coupling—stared into his, brimming, welling, bursting with joy. "That's it, fuck me. Fuck me. Fuck me, you stallion. Fuck me. Why do you"—she was gasping, panting—"think I invited you in? I wanted hard cock. Did you think I was gonna let you go to waste?"

Stretched, submitting, she rested her head to the side with closed eyes, groaning in rhythm with the thrusts of his thick dick deep inside her slick sex. "Harder, harder, HARDER!"

Pummeling, hammering, their crotches collided; slap after slap, as he plunged hard and fast, fucking with vigor, delving to her limits with power, determined rigor. He could feel his balls tightening, tingling; mouth open, her head was writhing, legs clamping, signaling. And then explosion came in unison, their screams mingling into crescendo as they released loud and proud their announcement of carnal conclusion.

∞∞∞

Stephen awoke the next morning nestled in cozy comfort. Both still naked, Isadora was awake and cuddled at his side. Gazing, smiling, she brushed his fringe with delicate flicks. "Morning, handsome. How did you sleep?"

"Great. This bed is awesome. The pillows too."

"Yea, although it's a lot more comfortable with you in it." She leaned forward and kissed his lips with soft skin and sincere affection. "So, I was thinking..."

"Yes?"

"Do you have to work at the spa today?"

"No, I took today off for volunteering. I should really be beating the streets right now."

"I see. Well"—she ran a light fingertip in circles around his nipple— "what if I made a donation to the kids' fund and you stayed here with me today instead?"

"Really?"

She squeezed into him tight. "Of course. How much do you normally collect in a day, on average?"

"Hmm about 100-150 bucks? It varies. 250 would be about the best I could do."

"Well, if you like, I can make out a cheque to your charity for 1000 dollars."

He jerked his neck back, smiling. "Really? Are you serious?"

Tutting, she tapped a light slap of mock rebuke on his chest. "Excuse me *young man*, do I seem like a woman without any money?"

"Well no, obviously—"

"Unless you don't want to spend the day with me..." she said with a pretend pout.

"I do, definitely. I mean if you're sure. It's a lot of money."

Her hand slid downwards, cupping his balls, rolling them gently in her palm. "Oh, you'll work for it, believe me."

The touch was so tender, caring. It felt amazing. "So, I'll be charity working, but from home, kind of?"

She giggled, caressing his hardening shaft. "Exactly. Think of all the good you'll be doing for people in need."

He pulled her forward into his strong embrace. "Well then, when you put it like that, I'd better get started."

Bonus

~Brazil, 2003~

Business was thriving in Brazil. No more so than at Balero Mining Co, the country's number one iron ore and nickel producer. Sitting at his desk, Eduardo was signing approval papers for the staff's Christmas bonuses. The amount—a result of his negotiations with the board of directors—was 5% of annual salary, but he could give up to 10% at his discretion. Hard work reaped rewards with him as the General Manager at company HQ.

And he believed in people getting what they deserved. All employees received extra money in their December paycheck, but he also made a point each year of choosing the top three workers and giving them personal commendations in his office. This time though, there were four sat outside: Augustinha, Izabel, Domingos and Olivia.

Loosening his green silk tie a fraction, he beeped the two air conditioning units a few degrees cooler then placed the remote next to his mug of iced coffee. Remnants of ice cubes floated in a slushy beige mix which he sloshed back, enjoying the cool, bitter wave washing through throat and torso. It wasn't the temperature in Rio de Janeiro that oppressed; it was the humidity.

A final flick and check of documents and he was ready to invite guests from the waiting area. Pressing the intercom button, he spoke to his secretary, Gardenia. "Gardenia, can you please send in Domingos?"

"Yes, Mr. Santos," she replied in radio-like rasp through the plastic box.

In came Domingos, wearing dirt-smudged engineer's overalls. 6'2 of muck, smile and muscle. Eduardo stood, having to look upwards a little to meet eyes. They shook hands and Eduardo sat, while Domingos remained standing, hesitant.

"Sit, my friend, sit." He gestured to one of the leather office chairs in front of the desk.

"I don't want to dirty your chair, Eduardo. These things"— he moved his eyes side to side across the grubby material— "are filthy."

Eduardo laughed. "Good, you know I don't trust the guys with clean overalls. Now sit, I insist. You want some iced coffee?"

"No, no thanks, but cold water would be great," he replied, easing into the seat; pulling the top of his clothing in and out to create waft. "It's like a sauna out there."

Another buzz and request saw Gardenia bring two chilled bottles of water. Smelling like crisp lemon squeezed onto sweet honey, her slender brown fingers curled around and clicked the tops, handing them to each man. "There you go, Mr. Santos." Hazel eyes beamed submissive grins under flirts of fluttering eyelashes. Eduardo watched healthy hips shift inside tight skirt as she left. Pity she was married.

"So, how was it down below? Any pressing issues?" He sipped, reclined, and ran fingers through his silky cinnamon locks.

"Things are going very well. I estimate production will be up 15-20% by early Spring."

"Fantastic. And a large part of that success is down to your efforts, so I've given you the maximum bonus I can. Twice the standard amount, as thanks for all the hard work you do. Thank you, my friend. I wish everyone here were as dedicated as you."

They chatted a little more, shook hands again, and off Domingos went. The smile had doubled in size.

Next in was Augustinha, the mailroom's trainee. Just eighteen years old, she was adorable in oversized glasses, delicate white cardigan, and lime chino pants. Eyes green, cheeks pink and hair dark blonde all combined to form the epitome of teenage beauty. He'd warned several male—including, sadly, much older—employees about inappropriate comments they'd made towards her. He'd admired Augustina's bravery for coming forward about it.

Gesturing towards a chair, he welcomed her with a smile. "Hi, please sit. No, I wouldn't use that one, it's needing a clean. Please, here, Augustinha."

"Thank you, Mr. Santos." She was shy; the pursed lips pushing cheeks upwards to form rosy dimples.

"Oh, you're welcome. Would you like something to drink? Iced coffee? Water?"

"Thank you so much, sir, but I've just had a drink."

"Ok, well I wanted to have you in to say you're a great worker and I'm giving you the maximum Christmas bonus. I know you've only been here eight months, but I feel you deserve it. You're a very hard-working young lady. Thank you so much for your dedication. Now, has everything been ok...?"

A row of polished pearls emerged between delicate lips. "Thank you so much, Mr. Santos. You're so kind. I really appreciate it. And yes, since you helped me, it's all been fine. Thank you." Emeralds twinkled coyly beneath polished lenses, simpering, suggesting. So silly, he was old enough to be her father. Flattering, but no.

A cheerful chit-chat later, the next employee was sat in front of him: Izabel, the head of human resources. A larger lady with—putting it in polite terms—ample development, she brightened the whole workplace with positive energy and laughter. With her in charge, Eduardo could count on sound judgement and speedy performance whenever HR tasks were required. She was a flirt too, but within boundaries.

"What can I say, Izabel? You're a legend. Thank you so much for your hard work. You deserve the biggest bonus I can give."

"You're welcome. And thank you so much...Eduardo," she replied, skipping her tongue along the top of his name like a smooth stone across a calm lake.

"Behave yourself, you're a married woman." They laughed. She gave a cheeky wave on her way out.

Which left Olivia as the last person sitting outside his office. He loosened his tie further and took a gulp of chilled water. The air conditioners were churning a steady flow of coolness, but his internal machinery was doing the opposite. Opening his desk's top drawer, he placed a file in front of him and sighed before asking Gardenia to send in the final employee.

And in she strode, parading a pretty face painted in happiness. Olivia was the head of accounting. She'd only been with the company for around two years, but they shared a solid rapport, and even a semi-spoken crush which—for reasons he wasn't sure of—had never been acted upon.

That was what made this so difficult for him. "So, Olivia—"

"Thanks so much for this, Eduardo. I wasn't expecting it. But I have been working hard, I can assure you." Her lips were coated in glossy crimson, plump, pouting; the skin was coffee with double milk.

"Well,"—he looked at the manila cover on the file, tweaking its corner between finger and thumb— "I didn't actually bring you here to talk about bonuses."

"You didn't?" Her voice pitched higher.

He opened the file. "The thing is, Olivia, it's been brought to my attention that there are...irregularities with some of the accounting."

"Oh?" The smile had been replaced by—what he knew was—feigned surprise.

"Yes"—he turned the pages around so she could see— "these figures show payments to contractors over the past year. Do you see?"

She was biting her upper lip. "Mhm."

Running his finger down the list, he stopped on a sum and tapped. "For example, this one. 2000 reals for window cleaning of our other buildings in Rio. You see?"

The deep swallow of someone holding their mouth open too long followed. "Yes…" Her voice was a croak.

"And these ones for four shipments of protective equipment to Florianopolis. Only two shipments were actually paid for. There are a number of these discrepancies. I've spoken to other members of staff and they've confirmed my suspicions. These payments were made for things that never happened, but the money disappeared anyway. Do you understand what I'm saying? I know what you've been doing." He took a deep breath and exhaled. It was surprising how heavy an invisible burden weighed on the ribcage.

Her hair was tied into a tight raven bun; she reached back and patted it. Eyes peeled with alarm, they roamed as if a plausible excuse could be found within the paint of his office walls or ceiling. And then liquid began welling in her lower eyelids. "I, I didn't mean—"

He could feel his patience evaporating. Blowing hard through pinched lips, he snapped, "If you try the waterworks routine, you're going to make me really angry ok? This is embezzlement, Olivia. You know damn well the government has a stake in Bolero too. That makes it even more serious. You could easily go to prison for this. I was looking for some kind of reason not to take it further. If you're going to insult my intelligence with tears —"

"Discipline me," she blurted.

"What?"

Her black satin blouse was stretched taut. She sat up straight, pushing her breasts out, causing the material to strain, creating small gaps between buttons. "Discipline me. Teach me a lesson. Eduardo, please. You can discipline me right now, then demote me, deduct it from my salary. Whatever you like. I'll do whatever you like. And then I'll never steal again, I promise."

He opened his mouth to scold her more, but stopped himself. Prickles of adrenaline surged in his stomach. Trembles coursed, from his toes upwards. He'd always found her extremely attractive. "You're single, I think?"

"Yes, *sir*. I'm single. Same as you..." She'd never called him sir before. He liked it pronounced with obedience from her moist, pink tongue.

"You realize what you did was wrong? You realize next time if you even so much as take a pencil home by mistake—"

"Yes, I understand sir. I was wrong and I won't do it again. Believe me."

An appropriate reward for actions rendered. He believed in that. Perhaps prosecution and probable prison was too harsh. He could administer his own punishment. It would be fairer. And he was starting to want it that way.

Standing, he walked past the polished oak conference table and opened the door into reception. The entire floor only held where Gardenia worked and his spacious office. "I'll be leaving early after I'm done here. It's just too hot for work, isn't it? Why don't you take the rest of the day off and go enjoy the beach? I bet the water's beautiful today."

Within three minutes, Gardenia was strutting down the corridor towards the elevator. When he returned to the office, Olivia was sitting with head hanging in—apparent—shame.

He'd been nice all year. Now an urge to be naughty was taking hold. After locking the door, he said, "Stand up."

She did as ordered. Her tapered waist and round thighs were wrapped in a black knee-length skirt. "And?"

"Take off your shoes and skirt."

Stepping out of her heels, Olivia reached back with both hands, unzipped, and shuffled, causing her skirt to heap on the floor around slender calves. She was wearing plain cut briefs, white with small red polka dots. Her thick thighs were toned, ending in pedicured feet and painted toes. His dick was stiffening. Letting out a sigh she stared at the floor asking, "Ok, what next?"

He tugged his tie off, placed it on the desk, and undid the top two buttons on his shirt. Pulling one of the guest chairs into the office's central space, he said, "Put your shoes and skirt in the corner, then get over my knee. I'm going to spank your ass until you regret every single real you stole."

She lay across his lap. Her ass—like most of those he saw while strolling along Copacabana Beach—was fleshy, like an overripe peach. Tucking his fingertips under thin cotton, he yanked the flimsy panties to her knees, causing flinch and yelp. "Shut up. You know damn well you deserve this."

Bare—and frankly, beautiful—her rear end was quivering, begging to be struck. Thieving little bitch. She was going to get it.

His hand landed in heavy smacks on soft skin. She began shouting, crying, "Ow! Ow! It hurts!" Slapping over and over, he watched as caramel cheeks flamed further towards scarlet with every scream she loosed. "Ow! It hurts! Ow!"

Yes, it did. A few more slaps like that and his palm would be pins and needles. Her uncovered vagina was pressed against him; he could feel warm liquid soaking against his trousers. The dirty little madam. There was a possible win-win solution available.

Rubbing her red-blotched bottom, he said, "You can have more spanking, or you can get fucked as punishment. I'll let you choose. Which is it?" His cock was swollen; the confines of boxer cotton and squash of her crotch were causing intolerable stress.

"Of course, fucking!" she snapped.

"Excuse me?" He tapped on tender cheeks, threatening more corrective action.

Voice deflating to a whimpering grumble, she replied. "Fucking. I choose fucking."

He stood, and she eased into a half-squat position, rubbing her bum, and looking embarrassed. "That was so hard. I thought you would be gentle. Can you please be gentler when you fuck me? Please? And please not in my ass. Please, Eduardo, it hurts so much."

Her fear of anal sex seemed genuine. Relenting, having expelled anger through spanking, he agreed. "I won't put it up your ass. And I'll be gentle."

"Thank you." On her knees now, she gestured with eyes to his crotch. "Shall I suck your cock? I'm good, I promise."

Laid flat on the conference table with his tiptoes touching the carpet, he was enjoying a Christmas bonus in blowjob form. She was stood over him, gurgling, gagging; trying hard to please, she gobbled his shaft right to the root. Her throat was full of pulsing mocha cock as she massaged his balls in her silky palm. He stroked her hair; it was difficult to be annoyed with someone who was giving so much pleasure. She hadn't lied about her skills, at least. Twisting tongue, caressing lips and drips of warm, wet saliva slipped and slid over every part of his privates. It was delightful.

But he was ready to penetrate. "Lie down here. I'm going to fuck you."

They swapped places. Spreading her legs wide, she pleaded, "Please don't cum in me."

"Don't worry, I'll finish on your tits. Unbutton your blouse, please."

After she'd done that, he pushed her beige bra up and over two large breasts; leaving the lacy material bunched under her neck. The nipples were erect, standing swollen like brown beads. She glared at him with hungry eyes and beckoning thighs. Some punishment this was turning out to be. He'd need to deduct a decent amount of salary instead.

Olivia was shaven below, except for a sliver of trimmed black landing strip. He pushed his cock—well-lubricated by her spit—between puckered lips. God, she was tight. Sliding as far inside as her passage would permit, they both let out a lingering sigh. Strong sexual connection, despite his disdain. She was no angel, but her sex was divine.

She held her legs open while he began fucking in steady, greasy slides. He was trying to plunge to the hilt, but—as happened with other women—his size meant around half the shaft was jutting no matter how deep he dug. Her pussy held him with slick grip as he screwed. She moaned, writhing on shiny wood, spread, subjugated; whining in delight, she ran manicured nails along his forearms in light scratching motions

Eduardo smelled furniture polish; synthetic sweetness blended with scents of sweat and sex. Brushing damp forehead with the back of his hand, he pumped harder into the bitch laid in front. She was taking everything he'd given with groans and gasps, grabbing his hips in attempts to devour more of the feast she was being treated to. Requests for gentle were faded, forgotten now his girth was causing stretch to such perfection.

Skin slapped, clapped; her big tits bouncing as their bodies bumped, she began grasping at them, clawing, teasing nipples with saliva-slicked fingertips. And then they moved to her clit, rubbing with purpose, agitated, rapid; squealing, growling, she was cumming.

Balls tightening, prick pulsing, he pounded faster; battering, raging, he grasped her thighs and delved, stabbing, raiding. Unable to contain, he withdrew, releasing jets of creamy goo across svelte stomach and chest. One string even reached her face, coating those crimson lips. She licked them clean. There was no more he could do.

∞∞∞

Dressed in her clothing and renewed confidence, she spoke in direct manner. "So? What else? Or was that enough to pay my debt?"

"Enough? That hardly seemed a punishment for you."

Tilting her head, she shrugged and formed a wry smile. "What did you expect?"

"Look, we'll work something out. Some deductions from salary, some unpaid overtime, and I'll leave it at that. Ok?"

"Thank you. Can I go now?"

"Yes, you can."

"Thank you, Eduardo." She walked to the door, unlocking it.

"And one last thing, Olivia."

Turning the handle, she looked back at him. "Yes?"

"I believe in second chances. I don't believe in third ones. I hope that's clear. Merry Christmas, and close the door behind you."

Espionage
~England, 1980~

Serenity was spreading. Every flake that fluttered was a tiny patch of progression towards the idyllic. Unrecognizable from only an hour before, the street Elizabeth looked onto had been transformed. Snow had an uncanny ability to paint its presence on any landscape and smother chaos through cotton coating. Cars, buses, bicycles, crowds; their traffic melted under each layer lathered from above. Arms folded, she leaned against the bay window's frame and breathed. So tranquil.

Which made her current task all the more perverse. She looked at her watch. Delicate silver slivers clicking around a rectangular face warned of time's invisible strides. No more to waste.

Turning her gaze into the large living room, she focused on its centerpiece. A man sat on a wooden kitchen chair. Blindfolded and bound, he was her captive. His tailored gray suit and silk tie made him appear so respectable, but sometimes the clothes did not reflect the man.

She took in the room once more. Furnishings in blue pastel, walls painted in mild lime. Vanilla candle fumes pervaded; an odd background scent for a job like this, but it was pleasant, nonetheless. The broad wooden bookcases—which reached halfway to the ceiling—were polished, packed with knowledge. A large oak desk sat in the corner piled with papers and stationary. Someone liked their study.

Yes, this was an unremarkable house in an ordinary location, the middle-class suburbs of London. The sort of place nobody would expect an interrogation to be taking place. Which made it so perfect. It was a nice street for nice people. And him.

She strolled across shag carpet, her high heels pressing between fluffy fibers as she approached the prisoner. "Now, I'm going to take off your gag, but if you shout out, you'll regret it, I can assure you. Is that clear?"

Frantic nods followed. Reaching behind, she untied the beige handkerchief which was wrapped tight between his lips.

Words blurted after he'd taken a couple of deep breaths. "There's been some sort of terrible mistake. I don't know who you think I am but—"

"There's been no mistake. And the problem isn't who I think you are, but who you think you are."

"Wha—What are you talking about?"

She looked at her watch again and sighed. "We're running out of time. Now why don't you start by telling me who you are."

"I'm Professor Kenneth Longman. This is my home. Whoever you are, you've made a mistake and—"

"Great"—she ran short fingernails along his cheek— "now why don't you tell me who you *really* are?"

"I just have. Can you take this blindfold off please?"

"Hmm...no. I don't think you need to see me. And I'm not here to follow your orders. It's the other way around, ok?"

"Please, you have the wrong man!"

"Well, that's a problem, because I'm 100% sure I have the right one. And I don't make mistakes when it comes to people like you."

"But I—"

"This'll be a lot easier if you drop all the pretense. Frankly, this professor persona bores me. As you know, the world is in the middle of a Cold War, and there's only room for one victor. I have limited time—and patience, be in no doubt—to find out everything you're hiding. Confess, and we can make this quick."

"I honestly have no idea what you're talking about."

She knelt and slipped the brown leather loafer and thin sock from his left foot, cupping the sole in her palm. His pale feet were smooth, warm; the toenails clean and clipped, he took care of himself. She began massaging, stroking. This wasn't in the rule book, but she liked to improvise.

"Does that feel good?"

"What the hell are you doing? You have no right to remove my clothing or touch me. Stop at once."

She sniggered. "I see. You're loathe to admit it. Well I know it does. And I'll tell you—"

"How dare you—"

"Be quiet! You have no idea what I'm capable of. Now, shut up. Do you know why having your foot massaged feels so good? It's because there are so many nerves"—she teased a fingertip across toes— "in here. Over 7000, in fact. They connect to every part of your body. Do you understand?"

"Yes, but—"

"But you see, whatever can give you pleasure can also give you pain. The stronger the heaven"—she pressed on the smooth bridge before giving it a light slap— "well, I'm sure you get my point."

"I don't understand what you want."

"I think you know damn well what I want. And the longer you keep up this bullshit charade, the angrier I'll get. You wouldn't like me when I'm angry."

"I don't like you now."

She smiled. It was ok, he couldn't see. "That's a pity"—

her voice lowered, softening to a whisper— "because I like you. You're a good-looking man."

"Am I?" He sounded genuinely surprised. At least he was modest if nothing else.

"Yes. If I'm nice to you, maybe you can help me in return?" She ran a hand the length of his thigh. The material was smooth, divided down the middle in crisp creases. Firm, strong legs too. Elizabeth could feel her panties dampening.

"I'm sorry, I'm married. I think this has gone far enough. Please let me go."

Rejection returned her tone to sternness. "I don't give a shit if you're married. Your wife isn't here now. And stop pretending you're innocent."

She undid his belt with angry jerking movements; his zipper rasped as she unfolded and spread the crotch of his pants in brusque manner, leaving his plain white underwear on display.

"Please don't. I'm so shy."

Laughing, she fumbled through the front slit, pulling cock through cotton, and letting it rest, filling her hand. Prime manhood under her power. She was beginning to soak below. "Oh, you have a big one. Your wife's a lucky woman. I hope she appreciates it?"

"Please, I feel so humiliated."

"An innocent man, eh?" She spat twice into her palm, spreading the bubbles around. "Let me tell you this: Nobody is innocent in this world." Fingers slippery with saliva, she began rubbing in a firm grasp. The flaccid flesh soon stiffened as she continued slick slides in ruthless rhythm up and down his veiny shaft.

She looked at the clock on the mantelpiece; this had to be done soon or it wouldn't be done at all. "Does your wife suck your cock?"

"Wha—No, she's a respectable mother of three. She doesn't

do things like that!"

"Doesn't she? That must be disappointing. Confess and I'll suck you off. Give you a real treat."

"I swear, I'm an innocent man."

Leaning forward, she placed her lips over the hat of his prick and pursed them, teasing with tongue in circular motions, pressing it into the slit. She pulled back to see his reaction; a glistening string stuck to her mouth, dangling from swollen cock head. It remained for a few seconds, then snapped as she continued to pry. "Anything to say?"

He was moaning, his breath had quickened. His voice was trance-like as he replied, "I'm sorry. I'm innocent. Please don't do that, I'm not used to it…it's too much."

Good. She placed him in her mouth again, deeper this time, feeling his thighs tense and twitch as she leaned forearms on them, working his cock in purposeful, long sucks. Slurping, gagging, tongue slid over ridge and vein; he writhed, wriggled, but not from pain. Her sex was now dripping.

Soft moans escalated to loud groans. He was responding. She'd get her confession, but might have to go a little further. She pulled his underwear to the side. Large balls bulged.

"My, these are fat, aren't they? Fat as ripe lemons. Doesn't look like your wife's been doing her duty."

"She's"—he gasped as Elizabeth rolled the furry sack's contents between fingers and thumb—"she's busy with our kids. She's a great mom. Please don't judge her."

"Admit it, you're not this so-called innocent professor. Admit you want to fuck right now while your wife's away."

"I don't"—she smooched and licked his sack, causing his voice to pitch high—"I'm"—

She gobbled both balls at once, sucking hard, knowing the strain it would cause. "Mhm?"

And then his hands were free. Grasping her hair, he pulled her head back. "Ok, you wanted me to confess. Fine. Let's do it."

He rocketed to his feet, tearing off the blindfold and dragging her towards the desk in the corner. She stumbled, sending a high heel tumbling across carpet into the corner. He was so much stronger than her. She was in for it now.

Sweeping the desk clean, he sent papers, pens and staples into flutter and rattle as he pressed her face on its polished chestnut surface. Her skirt was tugged upwards with such force it almost bunched at her armpits. He tore at her panties, ripping them in two. The material—now completely sodden—trailed around her ankles in tatters. Bare-assed and bent over; the tables had been turned.

And then he knocked her legs wide with his knee, exposing all below. Helpless, she felt his manhood being forced inside, filling her wet pussy. Grasping the desk, gasping, she loosed a yelp as cock plunged and retreated repeatedly in full lengths. The size shocking, her eyes strained in their sockets as he bordered on breaking limits.

Venomous whispers slithered at her ear, speckling it in flecks of hot spit. "This is what you wanted isn't it? This what you like right? And yes, I confess I'm not the innocent man I pretend to be. Now keep your head down while I fuck you."

Her head stayed down but the volume turned up. "Yes, yes, that's it! Fuck me! Fuck me!"

Elizabeth's hips were held in manly clamps as cock stretched and balls slapped. Her sex tingling, legs trembling; she began to squeal as his pace quickened, the bumps rapid, cock rigid. And he was laughing. "That's it, make noise. Scream all you like. Nobody's going to hear you."

So good, so good, she scratched at the wood, clawing; his grip unrelenting, hips hammering, she wailed and spasmed as his cock exploded into her dripping, quivering chasm.

∞∞∞

Collapsed together on the sofa, she snuggled into his chest as they recovered their breath, giggling. "Mmm that was so wonderful. I'm glad I didn't wear expensive undies though," Elizabeth said with a kiss on his smooth neck.

"Well if you pull a tiger's tail, honey," replied her husband, Prof. Ken Longman.

She giggled, drawing her fingernails down his shirt like a claw. "Yes, you were a tiger. Was amazing. I wish we could do this kind of thing more often."

Stroking her hair, he nodded in agreement. "Definitely. Especially this espionage one. It's my favorite so far. How about you?"

"Hmm, well, the police one was nice and so was the doctor's visit, but yes, I did really enjoy giving a spy interrogation."

He looked at his watch. "Quarter to seven. Your mom will be back with the kids soon. We'd better get changed and tidy up."

She shifted upwards and planted a strong kiss on his lips. "Yes, then I'll make a start on dinner. Merry Christmas, honey, I love you."

"I love you too, sexy secret agent."

Present

~Chicago, 2012~

Chrome glimmered as Imani barked directions along the barrel of a .38 caliber revolver.

"Get over there. No, not there. Yes, there. Now sit. Sit down on your ass. Put your hands behind the pipe and don't move. Don't make me shoot you."

"I uh—"

"Shut up."

She turned to her best friend, Jada. "Cuff him to the pipe. And make sure they're locked." Her gun stayed trained on the intruder.

Jada secured the man's hands around the thick iron heating pipe with two crisp metallic clicks, tugged the handcuffs to test, then grasped his black ski mask and whipped it off.

Silky blonde locks tumbled round the sides of a square-jawed, handsome face. Steel blue eyes wild; they darted, awkward. "Ladies, I—"

"Be quiet"—Imani kept sights centered towards his chest—"don't open your mouth unless I tell you to. I'm within my rights to shoot you, so you best be quiet. Are we clear?"

Adam's apple bobbed along with head; his tone sounded like one of restrained fear. "Yes."

With the pistol still stretched in his direction, she beckoned her friend. They took a few steps back and then turned to form a hushed huddle.

"Are those real cuffs? Or play ones?" asked Imani in a whisper.

"Real as can be. Remember that cop I dated last year?"

"You stole his cuffs?"

She shrugged and rolled her eyes. "Borrowed…"

Imani scowled, but was happy her bestie had these inclinations. At least for today.

"Ok good. Now let's call the cops."

Jada looked back at the burglar. Her eyes scanning from foot to forehead, she took out her phone and swiped it open. Manicured nails painted in purple; her fingers hovered over the screen in seeming hesitation.

"Hurry up. What are you waiting for?"

She didn't answer.

"So, did you steal anything?" Her voice was surprisingly soft, considering they'd come home only 10 mins before to hear him sneaking about in their attic, uninvited. The boards had given him away, creaking under his size. He must have been around 6 feet, and his thin black sweater was pushed tight with muscles. Imani was the one with the gun though.

"No ma'am, I didn't. And I'm sorry for—"

"Hush now, we'll work this out. Be quiet for now, there's a good boy."

She didn't like the way Jada was talking to this burglar. Gesturing with an agitated index, she drew her close. "Work it out? Good boy? This guy's a thug. What the hell are you playing at?"

Jada stifled a smirk. "He's no thug. Look at his face, his hair. Looks like he just walked off a damn movie set. Look at that body. Does he look like an addict to you? Gym addict, maybe."

Imani peered over Jada's shoulder. "Well, he does look good.

He—"

She raised her eyebrows. "Good? That's a fine piece of white ass, and you know it. All day at the mall you were complaining about not having a man, how much you want a man, how horny you are, why can't Santa bring you a man, and—"

Replying through bared teeth she said, "I didn't mean a fucking robber."

Jada took a lingering look at him, made a tiny snarl, and said, "I think we need to check if he's really stolen anything."

"You mean search him?"

A wicked grin appearing on her cherry lips; she shook her head. "Not just search. Strip search."

"Strip? I think we—"

Jada walked over to him, towering with hands on hips. She was 5'9, borderline plus size, with a large bust and thick arms. An imposing figure, especially to a man who was sat handcuffed from behind with legs stretched out over their varnished floorboards.

Her voice was becoming even softer though; the words oozing in silky syllables as she questioned. "So, uh"—she bent down and brushed his floppy fringe to one side—"what's your name?"

"Uh, Alec, Ma'am."

Imani walked around and sat on the wide arm of the chestnut leather sofa, where she had a clear line of sight towards the burglar. She kept the revolver pointed, but moved her finger from the trigger to underneath the cylinder. The vibe he was giving off wasn't menacing, more like apologetic. And, after seeing him closer, she couldn't believe how good-looking this thief was.

"Ma'am, eh? I like that. You keep calling me ma'am, ok?"

He nodded. His cheeks were pale pink roses speckled in blonde stubble. "Yes, ma'am."

Jada stepped back beside Imani and nodded with arms

folded. "My friend wants to call the cops. And why shouldn't we? You can't go breaking into people's homes. You scared the shit out of us. Why do I get the feeling a nice boy like you knows better? How old are you?"

"Twenty-five, ma'am. I'm so sorry, this was a big mistake. This is the first and last time I ever try to steal."

"Mhm. Is that so? Well you certainly won't be doing it *here* again, that's for sure. You do realise she almost shot you?"

"Yes, ma'am"—he looked at Imani— "and I'm so sorry for frightening you. Sincerely, this isn't me. I just..."

He sounded genuine. The heat of Imani's anger was sinking, from boil to simmer. "You just what?"

"Work's dried up at the moment. I was short on cash. I fucked up. I'm really sorry. Please don't call the cops."

"And what do you do, Alec?" asked Jada.

"I'm a model ma'am. Mostly underwear."

"You uh"—Jada sunk a tender bite into her lower lip— "you model drawers?"

Light blush in his cheeks strengthened to scarlet. "Yes, ma'am. And vests, bathrobes, that kind of thing."

The two ladies shared a look of bemusement, now the panic had subsided. After listening to the guy talk, it was clear he wasn't a thug. Tall and strong, certainly, but not aggressive or threatening.

Their living room was minimalist, open plan. She looked at the tree in the far corner. Branches decked out in tinsel, lights, baubles, and foil-wrapped chocolate treats—which Jada had been delving into daily—its base was piled with presents; their shiny paper sprinkled in pine needles. The conifer's sharp, refreshing fragrance was festive air freshener. Mixed with lingering scents of cinnamon incense, it invoked the spirit of Christmas.

She looked at hunky Alec and his ripped physique wrapped

tight in black. This was a bizarre situation, indeed. "Did you take any of the stuff from under that tree?" asked Imani.

"No, ma'am. I heard the front door opening and the back door was locked, so I climbed up to the attic. You came back only a few minutes after I got in. I haven't stolen anything, I promise."

Jada let out a humming "hmm" while scratching her fingernails softly over the sofa's leather. "Well, I have to search you in any case, sweety. Stand up."

The steel handcuffs scraped against the pipe as he stood straight. A fine-looking man. His broad, rippling shoulders and chest tapered down to a trim waistline.

Imani watched as Jada dipped a hand in each of his pockets. Nothing. Then she began unbuckling the man's belt. Her words had gone fluffy, coated in cotton wool. "You hiding something in here, Alec? Hmm? What you got hidden in here?"

Jeans pulled to his ankles; he stood only in boxer briefs. Topped with a thick black waistband, the red material clung tight, stretched over a pouch straining with masculine secrets. Imani's fizzling fury was reforming into reckless lust. She wanted to see what he was hiding. "Take his underwear down."

Hooking her fingertips inside the elastic at the top, Jada brought them to his ankles with one swift yank. She stood back to admire, giving Imani a clear view. Pale, purple-headed cock hung around the top of his sinewy white thighs. Thick and veiny, it stemmed from a porcelain crotch waxed smooth. Healthy man. She knew if it were slid inside, the size would have her stretched to the limit. Maybe Jada's approach wasn't so crazy after all. Dampness was developing.

"You got anything hidden at the back here?" Imani watched as Jada turned him and glided a palm over the bubble shape of his milky butt. Looked like one smooth ass.

"Please don't call the cops. I'll do anything if you let me go." His cock looked delicious, big balls too.

Imani lowered the gun. "Anything?"

He nodded. "Anything."

Jada stepped forward and stroked his blonde stubble. "You eaten black pussy before, hmm?"

"Sure, I'll eat your pussies. Just don't call the cops, ok?"

Imani could feel adrenaline spanking her stomach. This was scandalous. And she liked it. Resting the revolver on the sofa's arm, she walked close to him. His golden hair was beautiful, shining like fresh daffodil petals flowering from his handsome head. She rubbed her nose across his throat, catching notes of pristine powder, vanilla, and pepper. Spicy young man. "You'll eat"—she placed a gentle finger on his lower lip and pressed it up and down, enjoying its plumpness— "pussy. You'll eat ass. You'll do whatever we tell you. Ok?"

"Yes, whatever you like. I'll do a good job, as long as I walk at the end." The voice was calmer. Confidence was emerging in his tone. Imani got the feeling this boy had skills.

She picked up the gun again and gestured to it with her eyes. "My friend's gonna release you from the pipe, but the handcuffs will be staying on while you uh"—she stroked the barrel's side— "make amends for your behavior. Stay still now, ok?"

Jada was swift in unclipping the handcuffs, then re-locking them around his wrists, which remained behind his back. She fondled and stroked his bottom. "Work out a lot, don't you? Keep this nice and firm, huh?"

"Leave his pants where they are. Alec, get over here and go down on your knees. We're gonna make good use of our uninvited guest."

Underwear and jeans bunched at his ankles like makeshift shackles; he shuffled with ass bare and cock swinging to beside the sofa, then lowered as he'd been told.

Imani sat on the adjacent sofa. "You go first, I'll watch the show."

Fingers fumbling, Jada was unbuttoning her pants, saying with trembling tone, "Don't you worry, Alec, I'm gonna be nice and gentle with you. You just do as I say now, ok?"

Knelt, restrained and naked from the waist down, Alec nodded in obedience. "Yes, ma'am."

Once her lower clothing was off, she lay spread on the sofa. "Come here, Alec. Come to mama. We're gonna see how much sugar you got for me."

Taking hold of his head, Jada guided him onto her sex. Imani shifted so she could see the tonguing more clearly. Hands cuffed at the top of his luscious round ass; his head began bobbing as he ate Jada's pussy. She reacted with a look of shock upon first contact—no doubt adjusting to the sudden ecstasy—and then, moaning, sank back on squeaking leather with a long sigh; like slipping into a warm bath.

Eyes closed, she pouted and licked lips, moving her mouth as if savoring fine morsels. Her head was contracting back, in rhythm with the teases from Alec's raspberry tongue.

"Is he good?"

She ran fingers through his thick, golden hair. "Mmm. So good. He's a little sugar mouth. Boy is sweet." Opening her eyes, she stroked his crown, directing him. "That's it, sweety, get it in deep. Now lick the pink right there. Yea lick all that pink. Yea, you"—she drew breath hard through gritted teeth— "you found the spot. You know it. Press harder. Mmm that's it. Harder. Don't stop. You're repaying your debt to"—she let out a gasp and giggle — "society right there. Mmm."

Leather creaked, handcuffs clinked, the scent of sex mingled with pine and cinnamon as Alec slurped and sucked, lapping, gurgling, his tongue fluttering, and lips caressing. He was trying hard to please. Imani's panties were soaked.

She could see Jada's breath quickening; her knees quivering

as she held his head with both hands, fingernails digging through silvery sheen down to the scalp. "You lick that clit. Lick it. Fast as you—I'm gonna—fast as you can—I'm gonna, I'm gonna—don't stop, sweety! Don't stop!"

Jada's thick thighs wrapped and contracted as she spasmed to a standstill. After a few seconds stiff as a statue, she unwound, splayed on the sofa, panting. "All I can say is, Merry Christmas. Oh my, Merry Christmas, indeed."

Alec turned and looked at Imani. His mouth and chin shiny, he asked, "And now you?"

She sat forward. That cock was no longer hanging; it had risen proud, pulsating, swollen.

"Stay on your knees. I'll be right back."

Returning, she held up a puffy foil square with serrated edges. "I'd rather not use one of these, but you are a criminal. Kinda. Best be safe while I'm"—she tore the packet open— "having my way."

Jada was now standing in only panties, sliding a menthol from its box. Her lighter rasped and flamed before she blew a puff of mint-scented smoke into the living room air. "You're gonna fuck him, huh. Good. You need to get that out your system. Be all relaxed for Christmas tomorrow."

"But you didn't make him eat ass," Imani said as she slipped off her yoga pants and thong. Now naked below, she tutted, reached back, and pressed his face against her cheeks. "Eat."

Jada moved to the adjacent sofa, curling up, looking with sly eyes. The air was getting thicker as she blew rings of minty haze with lazy puffs.

"Get your tongue in there. That's it. Mmm. Yea. You do have a sugar mouth, don't you? Yea eat my ass. Try and push it"—the slither's strong sensation caused a gasp— "up the hole."

Wet, warm, probing; his wonderful mouth was turning drip

into flow. Knees shaking, the nerves around her ass were melting, sending courses of intense pleasure in every direction. She had to ride that thing. With no delay.

"Ok, lie back, Let's get you wrapped." Cream-colored latex was greasy against her fingers as she rolled it down his throbbing manhood. The condom struggled to reach the shaft's root. She pulled and pressed, making sure it was on securely. "Your cock's almost too big," she said in a lighthearted manner of scolding. Both the women laughed. Alec gave a bashful smile.

He was laid flat on leather as she perched. Holding his massive rod, she steadied herself onto it with care, nestling its tip between her folds before starting heavenly slide, one tender crunch at a time towards fulfilment.

Stretched full, she leaned far back, enjoying the paradise of pulses generated by their joined bodies. Her petit hands grasped his lower legs. Skin soft and muscle hard; Alec's calves were coated in silky blonde hair which rubbed with delightful soft scratches under palm.

Imani began fucking. Gyrating, she writhed her athletic hips in a corkscrew motion, trying to envelope every inch she could. With closed eyes, Alec's hands were still chained behind, but he was sharing heaven all the same.

She could hear Jada's voice, husky through blown smoke. "Yea, you work him, girl. Work that boy. Mmm, you ride him good. Santa didn't forget about you, huh." Turning as she rode cock; she saw Jada's eyes had settled into slits as she took long slow puffs and licked her lips. "Mhm, yea you enjoy that boy. Cock that size, no point in wasting it."

Guzzling, drinking; pleasure was pouring, but not from a cup, as taut leather crinkled, and steel tethers jingled. She slid her palms under Alec's top and rubbed warm abdomen, hard as steel. Guy was shredded. Going faster, her ass and thighs began to slap on his crotch as she fucked. Striding, colliding, slippery rubber squeaked as pleasure began to peak. This was sleazy, debased; all wrong, sinful, but so perfect, so right.

Alec's face was contorted, a handsome mask drawn in devilish delight. Quickening breath and bulging eyes told her his balls were about to unleash. "You can come, Alec. Don't hold back. I'm nearly there too."

Nodding, mouth agape, his words squeezed out in gasps. "Ok. Soon. I'm gonna."

Heat was building, ecstatic embers were feeding, crackling, fire was coming. The flames licking around her toes, growing, spreading like lava along limbs; her whole being on the brink of eruption. Spurting, she screamed as explosion struck. Lightning, thunder, galaxies ablaze in wonder, heaven crashing, smashing, the night sky pierced as she roared powerful and fierce.

"Nothing beats cock! I swear, nothing beats cock! This is the best Christmas present ever!"

∞∞∞

Alec was uncuffed and allowed to dress before having 100 dollars pressed into his back pocket and being pushed out into icy breeze and fluttering flakes. Imani barely had enough energy to stand as Jada spoke through a thin sliver of open door, shielding from the chill. "It's Christmas, sweety. A time of forgiving. Don't come back here though, ok? Or we won't be so lenient next time. Get some dinner with that. And Merry Christmas."

"Thanks for the cash."

"Thanks for the present."

Flight
~Flight EA875 to Dubai, Present Day~

So, this was Christmas. Fabulous. Diana had just been given the worst present possible: 2 weeks' notice of employment termination. Perfect.

Clicking her phone closed, she slipped it back inside her flight bag. As she was putting it in the overhead storage, a soft palm rubbed her waist.

"Hey, babes. Have you had any emails yet?" asked Kirsty, the other crew member attending to first-class.

Diana nodded, pursing her lips. "Yea. Just got it. 2 weeks' notice. You?"

Looking apologetic, she shook her head. "Nah, not yet. Shit"—she tutted through pristine pearls and plump strawberry pout—"that fucking sucks. Give's a hug."

Their abdomens pressed as completely as Diana's development would allow. Kirsty—aside from being the most gorgeous Irish crew member ever—was her best friend and roommate back in Dubai, where Emirati Airlines was based.

This was flight EA875 from London to Dubai, and it was shaping up to be her last time flying it, at least as an employee. The company was reducing staff numbers—or restructuring, as they put it—and a fresh round of layoffs had started a few days before. Notification—rather callously—was being sent by email, so crew around the world were in nervous wait to see if they would avoid being named in the unlucky lottery.

And she hadn't. Two whole days off awaited—Christmas and Boxing Day—and they'd be spent in a non-festive mood, that was for sure.

"We're still going out for a par-tay tomorrow though, right? You're not gonna let those bastards in HR ruin Christmas for you, surely?" Kirsty asked, leaning against one of the counters. Even in first class the galley area was functional; rows of metal box drawers and cupboards coated in plastic paneling with space for trolleys and a few slender asses to squeeze past each other.

Diana let out a sigh. "No, I suppose not. Last chance for Christmas in the sun, right?"

"Aww"—Kirsty leaned over and caressed her upper arm through thin white cotton— "maybe I can get Jack to bring a nice friend...?"

"Nice friend? You mean like last time?" she replied, raising an eyebrow.

"What? He was hot..."

"Aye, he was, and he went off with the waiter."

Kirsty shrugged, eyes cheerful and cheeky. "Was still hot. And he bought you drinks, at least."

Diana smiled. She was glad of her friend being there. "Very funny. But It's ok, please tell him I don't need a guy brought along. I'm happy to hang out with you two. You're getting the first bottle of wine though, seeing as you still have a job."

"Ha, the evening is young. Could be in the same position as you by the time we touch down. Could even get the email before take-off. I've only been here 6 months more than you."

"Yea, but you follow the rules better."

They both chuckled. Kirsty picked up the manifest on its clipboard. It listed everyone who would be on the flight. First class, which even on the colossal A380 consisted of just 8 private cabins, was rarely full. The cost of tickets was out of reach for most people.

Diana was hopeful the journey would be quiet and any arriving passengers not too demanding. "So, what's the story then? How many?"

"Oh. My. God."

"What?"

Kirsty pressed the board against her chest, guarding the information. "Ok so, who is the hottest man on earth?"

"Eh?"

"Who's the hottest man on earth?"

"What? Come on, you must be joking."

"Nope." She shook her head, causing bobbed blonde locks to sway in gentle knocks; sapphire blue eyes were sparkling above a delightful rascal's smile. Diana had been told a couple of times she was prettier than Kirsty, but it was hard to believe.

"You're really serious?" Diana was starting to feel adrenaline poking at her ribs, tickling along fingers and toes, evaporating sadness.

Energized, Kirsty turned the manifest around and gestured down. "See for yourself."

And there it was. His name: Levi Avery Benedict. Lead singer of her favorite band, Alpha Centauri.

"Oh my God. You weren't joking? It's really him!" They loosed squeals—albeit controlled ones—while Diana made tiny rapid claps with manicured palms.

"I know right? Holy shit. And he's the only passenger we've got too. I hope he's chatty, and—"

"Maybe I can get him to sign my nightdress? I've got an Alpha one in my bag," said Diana. The flight hadn't even taken off, but she was beginning to feel clouds collide against her head.

Kirsty's eyelids crinkled into slits, and she leaned close to whisper. Hot breath caused eardrum quiver as words oozed in spicy slither. "Maybe you should wear the nightdress when you ask him? He might sign your panties too. Maybe he'll even sign something else."

"Kirsty! You're terrible, really."

"What? I bet he'll love your Scottish accent"—she ran her eyes downwards— "amongst other things. I read he's single just now, too."

"I swear, you're terr—"

"Good evening, ladies. Permission to come aboard."

In their excitement, they hadn't realized people were boarding. Their only—and much anticipated—passenger was now stood on the edge of the first-class entrance in all his lofty glory.

Diana met his smoldering face with a stammered reply. "Hi th—Hi, Levi."

His square, stubble-peppered jaw broadened, the lips peeling to reveal immaculate teeth aligned in white. "Well hi back"— he stooped to peer at her shiny gold name badge— "Diana. May I come on board?"

She craned her neck, fawning. She'd seen him on stage from afar two years before; he was much taller now they were stood close. Diana was 5'9 even without crew heels, so not used to men towering. It was a nice change. "Of course, welcome. How are you, anyway?" Her smile was out of control, along with her questions.

He seemed amused. His charcoal hair flared in suave spikes, the eyes—delicious milk chocolate—smiled in empathy. "You're an Alpha fan then?"

"I'm your biggest fan," she blurted. A twinge of shame pinched her. Had she really just said that?

"Ah, I'm sorry, Mr. Benedict. We're both big fans. Welcome and please"—Kirsty turned to Diana, laying a gentle hand on her forearm— "allow my colleague to show you to your cabin."

Regaining composure, Diana led Levi through the plane. Each cabin was private, separated from the aisle by lockable sliding doors. They were essentially hotel suites in the sky, holding a large single bed, a connecting lounge area with leather sofa, coffee table and 40-inch flatscreen TV, and a private bathroom with shower. All wood was polished walnut and the bedclothes soft Egyptian cotton. She slid the doors open and explained the facilities.

"So, take-off will be in about 30 minutes. I'm sure you'll be comfortable. If there's anything at all I can get you at any point, please just push that call button on the sofa. There's also one next to the bed."

He sprawled on the sofa with one leg resting across the table. So tall. His designer sneakers glistened with golden studs and buckles. So stylish. He took off his jacket and dropped it in the corner, but Diana hung it in the private compact cloakroom, receiving gracious thanks. She liked him even more than before. His plain white t-shirt was drawn tight against marble torso; arms—sleeved in tattoos—bulged, twitching with vascular health. She wasn't sure what fragrance he had on, but it smelled like droplets of fresh citrus squeezed over a supercar's leather seats.

"Thank you so much, Diana, this'll be great. Now, can I please get a drink?"

"Of course, Mr. Benedict, there—"

"I think we're already on first name basis," he said with a smile and dismissive hand gesture.

"Oh, well, thank you so much, Levi. As I was saying, there's a mini bar just there, in the compartment under the table, but honestly, the good stuff is in the galley."

"Well"—he stretched, causing his t-shirt to shift upwards, revealing chiseled abs— "I'm a fan of the good stuff. Do you have cognac?"

"We certainly do. Remy Paradise. Shall I bring you one?"

He was unbuckling his sneakers, slipping them off to reveal large feet coated in black cotton. "Yes, please. Big one, Diana." His voice was beautiful. The tone melodic, soft, but with underpinning manliness.

"Of course. Shall I put your sneakers in the cloakroom?"

"So kind, thank you."

Bending to pick them up, she felt eyes on her chest. The white cotton blouse she wore was fastened fully, but always tight—despite being 1 size larger than her slim waist needed—and her sizeable assets tended to bunch when she bent forward, putting strain on buttons. She caught his stare. He smiled and looked away.

"I'll be back in a few minutes with your drink, *Levi*." There was a spectrum of softness with which to pronounce names. She chose a subtle tone in the scale.

"Oh, Diana," he said, as she was leaving.

"Yes?" Her smile was saccharin as standard for male passengers, but in this case, rich syrup coated her lips.

"Where are you from?"

"Perhaps have a guess? If you don't mind, of course?"

"No, that's ok." He frowned, nibbling his lip. "Hmm. Let me see…Scotland?"

"Yes, good guess! I normally get Ireland for the first guess."

"Well, the accents are similar—to be honest I was torn a little between Scottish and Irish—but I find the Scottish one more distinctive. More beautiful too. But I'm sure you hear that all the time."

She gave a gentle shake in coy disagreement. "Well, not really, but thanks." She did hear it a lot, but not from rock idols.

Diana all but skipped down the aisle. Soon to be unemployed, but loving the moment. She removed the bottle of cognac from its cabinet. Taking a crystal tumbler and beginning to ease out the bottle's cork to pour a measure, she stopped. Fuck it, she'd take him the whole bottle. The thing retailed at 2000 dollars, but what were they going to do? Fire her? They already had.

When she returned with the tray, he was still relaxing on the sofa, checking his phone. Cognac, tumbler, mini ice bucket, carafe of water and a teak bowl of warm nuts were placed on the coffee table.

Putting down his phone, he said, "Oh, you serve drinks by the bottle on this airline. Nice touch. Remind me to book again. And macadamias, too. My favorite"—he scooped a couple of the nuts and began devouring in hearty crunches— "awesome. Thank you."

"Well, its normally by measure only, but seeing as you're an extra special VIP, I thought you'd like to pour your own. And if you're hungry after take-off, you can order as many meals as you like. The menu's in that sleeve there."

Releasing the bottle's cork with a squeaky pop, he poured maroon spirit, letting it slide into the glass with gentle gurgle. "I might be hungry"—he stared into her eyes— "depends what's on the menu."

∞∞∞

Engines roared, plane soared; and with that, they were on their way to Dubai, humming over cloud tops, streaming through star speckled sky.

Once the seatbelt lights had pinged off, Kirsty and Diana were back in the galley, giggling about the rock royalty on board.

"It seemed like"—Diana shook her head and tutted— "nah, it's silly. Forget it."

"What?"

"Nah, I'm being silly, really."

Kirsty bared her teeth in mock anger. "You want me to strangle you? What?"

"It seemed like...he was hitting on me."

She rolled her eyes and looked Diana up and down. "Why the hell wouldn't he? You're fucking gorgeous, honey."

"Yea but come on, he could have anybody. I don't think—"

"Get your phone, let's go see him."

"Kirsty..."

"What? We're getting some photos. You said he's friendly, he won't mind. Get your phone."

The doors were still open when they arrived outside his cabin. Cognac in hand, he was sipping, watching the news on TV, and munching nuts. The ornate crystal bottle was almost full. This wasn't the wild child portrayed by the media.

"Hey ladies, what's up?" Sat forward on the sofa, his arms— huge, patterned in roses, dragons, and a dozen other depictions— were toned and bulging as he fished another nut from the bowl. He was effortless sex on long, powerful legs. She scanned his strong-looking hands: No wedding ring. The most desirable bachelor on earth.

"So sorry to disturb you, Mr. Benedict, but would you be ok if we took some pictures with you?" asked Kirsty with an enquiring smile. She had a face that persuaded men to say yes.

"Sure, course," he mumbled through macadamia. Then he put a fist over his mouth, swallowed, and spoke with clarity. "How do you want me?"

"Whatever's most comfortable. May I sit beside you?" asked

Diana in feigned nonchalance, trying to mask tremble in her tone.

He patted the cushion of luxuriant Italian leather beside him. "Of course, please."

Diana perched, wanting so much to lean back into him. Readying the phone for photo taking, Kirsty wrinkled her nose, talking to Levi as if about a toddler. "She wants a cuddle, but I think she's too shy to ask."

"Kirsty!" Glaring at her friend, she turned to Levi, softening her tone, feeling sheepish. "I'm sorry, you don't—"

He shuffled forward. "Why not? May I?"

"Oh, sure, if it's not a—"

His arms wrapped around her waist in firm grip, the forearm tops brushing underneath her ample chest. Rugged stubble grazed delicate cheek, like divine sandpaper. She felt like they were a couple posing for a honeymoon shot. He whispered in her ear, the vibrations shooting tingles across scalp and neck. "That's beautiful perfume you're wearing. Suits you." The embrace was so enchanting, his strength so reassuring, comforting; she wanted it to go on forever.

Then Kirsty had a photo taken, but standing beside him with both thumbs up and beaming grin. Levi hadn't suggested a cuddle —she wouldn't have anyway, being fiercely loyal to Jack, her boyfriend—and his gaze was fixed on Diana. Was he toying with her? She was feeling something more than physical attraction.

∞∞∞

Club sandwich, fries, and cola. That was what Levi had ordered for dinner. Some of these rich passengers could be so picky, persnickety—to the point of pain—over food and drink. She adored his refreshing simplicity.

Holding the round plastic tray in one hand, she knocked on his cabin's closed doors. "Mr. Ben— Levi?" It still felt strange using his first name, but he had insisted.

She heard the hiss of fast flowing water. He was freshening up, so might not be able to hear. Knocking again, louder, she raised her voice. "Levi? May I come in? I've brought your meal."

"Yea, it's cool. I'll be out in a minute. Come in, and please wait for me."

No arguments about that.

As she was placing the tray, shifting the cognac and other items to make space, he emerged from the bathroom. Oh my. With only a towel wrapped around diamond-cut abdominals, his whole upper body was on display. Considering its miserable start, the flight was yielding relentless treats.

It wasn't ladylike to stare, but his physique was magnetic, drawing her vision despite notions of decorum. The shoulders —broad as a wardrobe—were set with sinew and smothered in striking tattoos. Contrast between ink and milky pink was delightful. Pectorals rippled in perfect definition. He was a legend lifted from Greek lore. Achilles, Perseus, Hercules, Hector; she wondered if any of those heroes could have compared to the masculine statue stood before her.

"So, I was wondering"—he took a section of the club sandwich, wolfing the chunky triangle in one bite— "if you would like to hang out in Dubai?" Talking with his mouth full. Rude boy. But she didn't mind.

"For Christmas?" The answer was going to be a big hell yes.

Levi swigged cola, releasing a satisfied gasp. "Yea, I mean I don't know what plans you've got, or if there's somebody expecting you...?"

He was eating but she was feasting. Running her eyes over his body—and doing so in deliberate fashion—she replied, "There's nobody. And"—she smiled, gazing at his face, feeling her neck quaking— "I'm flexible about plans. If you have something in mind?" She wanted to touch, taste, lie cradled in his arms; cravings were consuming, but how to deal with them?

And then the Gods intervened. The plane, which had been cruising in serenity for hours, struck a pocket of turbulence, jolting the whole cabin, causing the floor to shudder, and sending her careering forwards. Into his embrace.

As everything around them shook, he held her tight against his chest, solid, not budging. Face pressed against smooth stone, she smelled coconut and lemongrass. Standard body wash in their first-class bathrooms, but on him it was tropical paradise; palm leaves in balmy wind were swaying in her nostrils as wind battered and aircraft jostled. Her panties were dampening, and breath quickening as they braced against the elements' brief show of force.

The disturbance eased. At least, the one from outside did. Internal turmoil continued churning. Still wrapped in his arms, she looked down. The towel was heaped at his feet. He was completely naked.

She stepped back, not saying anything. Neither did he. There was no need. Silent understanding—bred by strength of chemical connection—was all the communication necessary. Levi made no attempt to cover, and Diana felt no shame in looking. It was what they both wanted.

Staring in disbelief, she marveled at his cock. The pubis waxed smooth; its thick, flaccid shaft reached far down his thighs. A bulging sack hung underneath. Those balls, the length; he could have populated a small country with his blessings. She was glad of the spare underwear in her flight bag.

Levi shrugged, sporting a cheeky grin. "Sorry. Turbulence, eh? What can *we* do?"

Now soaking under her skirt, she nodded. "I'll be back in a few minutes."

Striding down the aisle with purpose, she found Kirsty lying across two crew seats, playing games on her phone. Drawing close, Diana gestured up the staircase and whispered, "Has Elsa been down much?"

"Nah, she popped down earlier for a few minutes. Said she would be 'doing paperwork in her office'"—Kirsty sniggered—"aka napping and tippling on the good gin. Why?" Her eyes were smirking, as if she suspected the answer.

"Because I'm going to"—she gritted her teeth and made clear the code—"spend time with Mr. Benedict."

Kirsty's mouth gaped. "Oh my God, you are gonna. Holy shit, that's fucking awesome."

"Thanks, bit nervous, sweety." She was seeking reassurance more than commendation.

"Don't be silly, just go for it. I've got you covered, ok? Shit, have you got condoms?"

"One in my purse. Will have to do. Hope it fits him." She parted her palms, gesturing like an angler boasting of a prize catch. They both stifled raucous laughter.

∞∞∞

Levi was still standing naked when she returned; hands on hips, huge cock hanging, muscles bulging. Breathing sped and heart hammered as she clicked the double doors locked, ensuring privacy. This was happening.

He came close, dwarfing her, and then—to Diana's surprise—lowered to his knees. After removing her shoes, he reached his arms around her waist. A metallic rasp signaled her skirt zip had been undone. Giving the material a gentle tug, he helped her step out, folding and tossing it on the sofa. Her lower half was now only covered with cream crew tights over pink frilly panties. Wet ones.

He began kissing the nylon, caressing knee and thigh with soft palms and strong fingers; his hands rubbing in circles, rising higher towards her beckoning sex. Upwards. Further. Every inch ecstasy. Nerves were alight in lustful delight.

She rested her back against the doors, gasping. Running fingers through his soft hair, she stroked his ears, playing with the lobes, massaging with gentle grasps while he pulled tights and panties to her knees, exposing her dripping sex.

And then she was naked from the waist down. Cool air teased from heel to hip while soft carpet fibers pressed bare soles; the hem of her blouse hung too high to hide shaven secrets pink and puckered. Watching his bubble gum-colored tongue inching towards her pussy, she whispered, "Let's go in the bedroom and close the doors. I'll make too much noise. The whole plane will hear."

He smiled, nodded, and stood. As she walked towards the separate bed compartment, he landed a playful smack on her bottom. Not painful; a sting of perfect sparks. Turning, she grinned and said, "Oh, it's like that is it?" Returning the favor; her slender palm whacked his behind with a gentle slap. And then, unable to resist, she groped his ass in greedy handfuls. It felt like satin stretched over granite.

The closed bedroom doors made her more comfortable, but she was still aware of the potential for reverberating sounds. Rubbing his stubbled cheek, she said, "We're both gonna have to be careful about noise. If people hear, we could get in deep shit. Trust me, the Dubai police don't fuck around."

He held up a tattooed forearm. "Bite the pillow or bite me, it's all good. I'll keep my mouth full"—he stared at the swollen bumps under her blouse— "in other ways."

They embraced again. Standing on top of his feet—in a futile attempt at height equality—she asked in mock annoyance, "Why are you so tall?"

Levi shrugged and answered with a kiss. A probing one. His tongue plunged, rubbing against hers in moist, tender twists. Lips spread wide, they tasted, fed, gorged; devouring, jaws joined in rhythm, they explored unmapped worlds within each other's warm, welcoming mouths.

Drawing her into a cradle of dominance, she reacted with simpering submission and began unbuttoning, enjoying his obvious anticipation. Tossing her blouse and E cup bra on the floor, she stood back for inspection. Regular pool time under the Dubai sun had shaded her Scottish skin a faint caramel, but her breasts—always being under a bikini top—were still pale white inside the tan lines. She'd now joined him in total nudity.

He shook his head in apparent wonder. "You're amazing. Absolutely amazing."

You're amazing. Not they're amazing. Not your tits are amazing. *You're* amazing. Those words struck her like a barrage of diamond bullets between the eyes.

"You're amazing too. Utterly amazing. Now"—she cupped her tits, offering—"what are you waiting for, handsome?"

Levi lunged, suckling with gluttonous gasps. Saliva soon coated her nipples and areola, causing milky glisten as he gobbled, licked, and kissed. Diana was primed, ready. Holding his earlobe in soft clamp between her teeth, the statement was blunt: "I need that cock inside me. Right now."

She unraveled the condom down his shaft. It fitted. Barely.

Pulling back pristine cotton sheets, she lay on the bed. Spread. He took gentle hold of her thighs, widening them further as he guided his twitching length between her legs. "You've got such a tight little slit. I hope I can get in."

"I'm so wet, you'll get in. Just go slow, be gentle please. I've never"—she gazed at his cock— "with somebody that size before."

He gave a reassuring smile. "Don't worry, beautiful."

Beautiful. Warm glow erupted in her stomach, washing down her legs and toes. He was the beautiful one.

Levi began his tender slide, causing both shock and delight to her quivering insides. She gasped, slapping the wall hard. Thank God the adjoining cabin was empty. "Oh God, God. I'm stretched. I'm fucking full. I've never felt so full." She looked down. He was fucking in firm, slow rhythm. And half his shaft was still visible. Wanting her body to take more, she rubbed his muscled thighs, trying to drag him forward, to envelope more masculine heaven.

Lifting her foot, he planted warm kisses on pale, painted toenails. "It won't fit any further, honey."

Honey. The word trickled into her ears. Levi Benedict was calling her honey. She'd do the same.

Groaning, growling, clawing at the sheets; she closed her eyes and drank in the divine, floating through starry night sky coupled with a demi-god as he burrowed and writhed in the wanton depths of her womanhood. Jet engines rumbling, his silky crotch slapping, pumping, faster, firmer, deeper, it was too much; she grasped at one of the sweat-dampened pillows under her head, turning its chunky white corner, trying to snare it in her mouth.

Voice pitching higher, feeling pressure building, her pussy crackling, tingling; she pleaded with Levi. "Honey, if I don't bite that pillow, I'll scream this fucking plane out of the sky."

Still fucking, he reached forward and placed his chiseled forearm against her lips. "Never mind the pillow. Bite this."

"Honey, I'll bite hard. I can't—"

"Trust me, I've got a high pain threshold. Bite it."

She placed teeth on tattooed skin in soft clamp. And then he started hammering. Hips belting, pounding, pummeling, his rampant vigor sent nerves reeling as she sunk jaws into flesh, tears welling from streams of frenzied squealing.

While earth and ocean whizzed below, Diana was rocketing. Knocking planets, battering moon and sun, her thrashing legs smashing stars to glittering golden shards, their showers cascading, waterfalls of dazzling wonder swamping her entire being as all feminine essence released, gushing, heaving.

Opening her eyes, still in the sky, still alive despite having died, she returned to Levi, now collapsed, panting, lying at her side.

∞∞∞

She lay huddled in Levi's embrace as they looked through the window at golden twinkles bunched and sprinkled among the darkness below.

"Any idea where we are?" he asked while peering at the passing lights.

"Yes"—she kissed his hand and turned—"heaven."

He stroked her cheek. "That goes without saying. So, you'll spend Christmas with me then?"

Rolling her eyes, she smirked and planted a firm smooch on his smiling lips. "Of course."

"And what do you want from Santa?"

She clasped his arms around her tighter. "Just you, honey. Just you."

∞∞∞

Diana never flew first class again, after her job ended. At least, not as a crew member. Her and Levi were married the following month, bringing into the world a number of beautiful, smiling babies over many fruitful years.

In time, she became a celebrity in her own right, establishing successful sports clothing and nutritional supplement brands as social media's most popular fitness model and diet guru. With help from her glamorous business partner and friend, Kirsty.

Life was one of excitement, challenge, and adventure, with Christmas always being her favorite time of year.

Sincere Thanks

Dear readers

Thank you so much for taking the time to read my work. I hope it brought you some enjoyment.

Please take the time to leave a review on Amazon and/or Goodreads, as this feedback is invaluable not only for me but for other readers who may be thinking of purchasing this book. Your help is greatly appreciated.

I wish you all Merry Christmas and a Happy New Year!

Sincere thanks

Florian

Printed in Great Britain
by Amazon